For Katie Livesey

First published in 2012 in Great Britain by
Barrington Stoke Ltd
18 Walker Street, Edinburgh, EH3 7LP

www.barringtonstoke.co.uk

Copyright © 2012 Robert Swindells

ISBN: 978-1-84299-768-0

Printed in China by Leo

Dan's War

by

Robert Swindells

Contents

Chapter 1
Well and Truly Bounced

Dan Langley's mum came out of the kitchen and shouted up the stairs. "Are you up, Daniel? It's seven o'clock."

"Yes, all right, Mum," growled Dan. "I'm coming." It was February, still dark outside. Cold too. *And* it was a Saturday. Dan's pals would still be snoring in their beds, the lucky blighters.

Still ... Dan looked at the photo of his dad on his bedside table. Able Seaman Langley, in uniform. Dan's pals still had dads. Their mums didn't need them to bring money into the house. Able Seaman Langley had died the year before last. He'd drowned in the icy waters of Scapa Flow. Now his mum had no husband and almost no money. "But she's got *me*, Dad," he told the photo. "We carry on all right."

His mum had made porridge for breakfast. Dan wasn't keen on porridge. He dreamed of sausages and bacon, but this was 1941. There was a war on. There wasn't much bacon and sausages, they were just in your dreams.

Dan and his mum sat hunched over their steaming bowls. "What time does Mr Pincher want you, love?" asked Mum, passing Dan the milk.

Mr Pincher was the gardener at Winton Hall. That was where Dan worked at the weekends. He was Mr Pincher's helper in the garden.

"Eight," said Dan. "Dunno what he wants me to do this time of year. Not a lot to do in a garden in February. Scratching round *looking* for jobs, mostly."

"Well," Mum smiled sadly. "It's lucky for us he's kept you on all winter, Daniel. I don't know what we'd do without your four shillings a week."

Dan shook his head. "It's not *Pincher* keeps me on, Mum – *he* doesn't decide. General Winton must've told him to."

"Well, you must be a very hard worker, love – the General wouldn't be paying you if he wasn't getting his four bobsworth."

They ate their porridge, sipped hot tea. Dan wished Dad was here to crack some jokes. Dad was good at jokes – knew hundreds. Now they were as hard to find as bacon. Dan wanted to tell Mum he was missing Dad, but he daren't. She'd start crying, and he never knew what to do when she cried.

It was two minutes to eight when Dan got to Winton Hall. He biked up the drive, between the stone gate-posts and scrunched up onto the gravel. It was cold, starting to get light. He could see Mr Pincher, bending near the stove in one of the glasshouses. He went over, stamping his feet to try and get warm.

"Nice and warm in here, Mr Pincher," Dan said.

"Ah," grunted the gardener, "but I'm not keeping *you* under glass, so you needn't think it. There's nowt like heavy digging for getting you warm, and the long bed in the kitchen garden needs turning. You'll find a spade in the shed."

Dan grinned. "Dig for victory, Mr Pincher, is that it?"

The old man gave a shrug. "Dig for owt you fancy, boy," he growled, "just as long as you dig."

The long bed wasn't called long for nothing. It was twenty yards from end to end, and it wasn't narrow either. Digging it was going to be hard work and boring. Dan gave a sigh, stuck the spade into the sticky soil and escaped into one of his dreams. Digging's the sort of job you can dream your way through, once you're into a rhythm.

Dan's dreams were all about the war. Like every boy of thirteen, he longed to be in it. He had Navy dreams, Army dreams and RAF dreams. This one was an RAF dream.

It's a summer's morning at an airfield in Kent. Squadron Leader Dan Langley strolls towards his Spitfire. His parachute pack bangs against his legs as he walks. 'Lucky' Langley has two bravery medals already. He's downed 69 enemy aircraft and has nothing left to prove.

He takes off. Five minutes later his plane levels off at 9,000 feet. His sharp eyes search the skies. Beware the Hun in the sun. He smiles thinly to himself. Nobody bounces Lucky Langley. Nobody.

A voice comes over the radio. "Twenty plus bandits over Deal, angels one-five, heading north-west." Langley smiles, turns the plane south-east. Twenty plus. This'll be a good fight – just him and twenty enemy planes.

The voice comes again. "Stop leaning on that spade and start digging, you lazy young hound." The Spitfire vanishes, the joy-stick's just a spade. Mr Pincher's the Hun in the sun, and Dan didn't see him coming.

'Lucky' Langley is well and truly bounced.

Chapter 2
Dig, Don't Count

At one o'clock, Dan stopped digging. He used the spade to scrape mud off his boots, then set off towards the glasshouses for his lunch. Mr Pincher might be a bit of a slave driver, but there was always something in his packed lunch for Dan, and he always put a billy of tea on the stove.

They sat on sacks of peat. The gardener took out his sandwiches and looked inside the top one. "Cheese," he grunted. "It were cheese yesterday, *and* the day before. Anyone'd think there was a war on. Here." He held out the paper packet of sandwiches to Dan. "Help yourself."

Dan took a sandwich. He was starving and didn't care what was in it. "Thanks, Mr Pincher." The gardener looked at him. "How far'd you get, boy?"

"'Bout half-way I reckon. I'll finish it before dark, bit of luck."

"Better do. General don't pay you to lean on the spade, dreaming you're a hero."

Dan looked at him. "How did *you* know what I was ...?" he began.

"Dreaming about?" Mr Pincher chuckled. "'Cos I had the same dreams in 1914, boy, that's why. Couldn't wait to get to France, have a go at the Hun. Then my dream come true."

"And what was it like, Mr Pincher?" Dan asked.

"Eh?" The gardener bit, chewed, stared at the glasshouse floor. Dan waited. A minute passed. Mr Pincher swallowed and reached for his tea. "Nowt like my dream, I can tell you that. Mud. Half frozen mud, up to your knees.

Then there was lice and rats, and dead bodies stacked up to make part of the trench wall. The shelling never stopped and there were snipers, and going over the top where the barbed-wire was waiting." He took a swig of tea, shook his head. "It's nothing like they tell you, boy. They said we was fighting the war to end wars and look – twenty years on and we're at it again." He sighed. "Your best plan, boy, is to pray it's over before you're old enough to go."

Dan's legs and back were stiff because he'd sat down. He felt even less like digging now, but it had to be done. *Anyway, it's better than standing in mud, being shot at*, he told himself as he plodded back to the kitchen garden.

As Dan passed the kitchen door it opened and Sal Barley came out with an enormous basket of washing. Sal was in Dan's class at school. Her mum worked at Winton Hall, and Sal helped her on Saturdays.

"Here," Dan said as he stopped. "Let me help." He held out his arms for the basket. Sal swung it away from him. "Don't you *dare* put your muddy paws on my washing, Dan Langley. Think I want to do it all again, do you?"

"I was trying to help, Sal, that's all," Dan said.

"Thank you, but I don't need help." Sal looked up at the sky. "Unless you can keep it from raining."

Dan watched the clouds. "I'll see what I can do, Sal." He turned round and went on to the half-dug bed. Sal took the big basket of washing to the lawn. As long as they kept their voices loud, they were close enough to talk as they worked, and they did.

"*Three pegs to every sheet*," growled Sal as she pegged a sheet to the line. "Mrs Burton's rule, that is. We only use two at home, but still."

Dan nodded. "They like their little rules, don't they? Mr Pincher's is, *it's not dug till it's dug deep*."

"What does *that* mean, Dan?" Sal asked with a laugh.

"Means you've got to shove the spade right down, like this." Dan showed Sal how Mr Pincher liked him to dig.

"It's all right for *them*, isn't it?" said Sal. "They don't have it to do."

They worked in silence then, till the long bed was nearly all dug over and seven sheets swung snapping on Sal's line. Dan watched them as he took a few minutes rest. "Hey, Sal, there's just the General living here, isn't there?"

Sal took three pegs out of her mouth. "How d'you mean, Dan?" she asked.

"Sleeping here. It's just the General isn't it?"

"And the housekeeper, that's Mrs Burton," said Sal. "She lives in."

"Two people, then." Dan frowned. "So why seven sheets? You'd expect four at most, wouldn't you?"

The girl shook her head. "There's the guests, Dan. The General sometimes has guests."

"Does he?" Dan made a face. "I've never seen any. Where do they come from?"

"Don't ask *me*," said Sal. "I'm a weekend maid, not the General's social secretary. Why should I know who he has to stay? They come by train, I suppose."

She picked up the empty clothes basket. "I'm off now, remember to keep the rain away. See you at school."

It was coming in dusk when Dan turned the last spadeful of earth. He scraped his boots, cleaned the spade and put it back in the tool-shed. He was looking forward to tea by the fire with Mum.

"Done?" grunted the gardener, when Dan walked into the glasshouse.

Dan nodded. "All done, Mr Pincher. Spade's away." He grinned. "I'll be away myself if that's all right."

"Just a minute." Mr Pincher looked at him. "There's more to working for someone than just the work, boy."

Dan frowned. "How d'you mean, Mr Pincher?"

"I mean, there's minding your own business," Mr Pincher went on.

"B ... but I *do*. I haven't ..."

"Counting sheets, boy. Did I tell you to count how many sheets on the washing line?" Mr Pincher asked.

"Well *no* Mr Pincher, but me and Sal were just chatting. I wasn't ..." but Dan didn't get a chance to finish.

"You wasn't minding your own business, boy," Mr Pincher said. "That's what you wasn't doing. If you want to keep your place here, dig, don't count. All right?"

"Yes, Mr Pincher. Sorry," Dan said.

"All right boy, you can go. Eight o'clock sharp tomorrow, mind."

"Yes, Mr Pincher."

Chapter 3
The Home Guard

"Walk round the house before you come in, love, and check the black-out's all right," Dan's mum called out when Dan got home.

"Aye aye, Mum," he said. He walked round the house to scan every window. No light showed through the heavy black-out curtains.

"It's fine," he reported and dropped his jacket at the foot of the stairs. "What's for tea? I'm starving."

"Stuffed cabbage," said his mother, "in a cheese sauce, with mashed potatoes."

It was a boring meal but Dan wasn't going to complain. He knew Mum tried her best to make nice meals for him out of their dull rations.

He ate everything on his plate. "That was wizard, Mum," he lied. "I was ready for it as well, after all that digging."

His mother smiled. "They say hunger's the best sauce, love," she said.

"What does that mean?"

"Means *anything* tastes good if you're hungry enough," said his mum.

He shook his head. "No, Mum, it *was* good. I mean it. Any afters?"

His mother made a face. "Semolina with prunes. You're so hungry it'll taste just like fresh peaches and cream."

Over the semolina Dan said, "D'you think they'd let me join the Home Guard, Mum?"

"Hmm – I think you have to be sixteen, Daniel. And anyway, I expect you'd lose your job at the Hall if you joined – the General doesn't like the Home Guard."

Dan frowned. "Doesn't *like* them? What's wrong about some chaps who are training to fight if the Germans land in England, Mum?"

His mother shrugged. "Don't ask me, love. All I know is, when the Little Billington battallion was being formed here last year, they asked the General to be its Commanding Officer. He said no. And he wouldn't let them train on any of his land either. That was hard for them because you know he owns half the village. He made a lot of enemies because of that – not that he didn't have plenty of enemies already."

Dan nodded. "No one likes the General. Did he do something *bad* in the last war, Mum? Some of the chaps at school reckon ..."

"Yes, Daniel. There was a battallion of local boys in the Great War. The Little Billington Pals, they were called. General Winton was their Commander. One day he ordered them to leave their trench and walk towards the enemy. A thousand started out, walking into machine-gun fire. A *thousand*, Dan – almost every young man in the village. They never made it. When at last another officer told them to stop, 770 of them were either dead or wounded. My dad – your Grandad Terry – was among the dead. That's why you never met him. Those boys never stood a chance. A lot of people in Little Billington think the General as good as murdered them. And on top of all that, he said nice things about Hitler a few years back. That was before the start of the war, but still."

"Crumbs." Dan shook his head. "No wonder no one likes him. Was Mr Pincher in the Pals, Mum?"

"Yes. He was one of the lucky ones. He got shot in the hand. They sent him home and he never went back to the front. He couldn't operate a gun any more. That's why he's alive today."

"And working for the chap who sent his friends to their death," Dan said in a low voice.

"Well, yes, Daniel. Everyone has to earn a living."

After tea they did the dishes, then listened to the radio. After the nine o'clock news there was a talk by a famous writer. The writer's

16

city had just been bombed, and he'd walked round it afterwards to look. Apart from a few burnt-out buildings, he said, everything was back to normal. People were carrying on as if nothing had happened. That's why Hitler would never defeat us, he said.

"Cheerful note to go to bed on," smiled Mum as she switched off the radio. "I'm tired out, I hope there won't be a raid tonight."

Chapter 4

Spam

"South lawn today boy, heavy roller." It was Sunday morning, eight o'clock. Dan looked at Mr Pincher.

"Heavy roller?" He grinned. "Is the General planning a winter cricket match or something?"

"Never you mind what the General's planning," growled Mr Pincher. "I told you yesterday – do your job and mind your own business."

Dan had never worked on the south lawn.
There was an orangery built onto that side of
the house, but it was empty now. Its glass was
dirty and cracked in places. When he peered
through, all he could see inside was a tiled
floor and some broken tables and chairs.
Shame, Dan thought. *The General could grow
his own fruit in here. Bananas, even. I'd kill
for a banana.*

The heavy roller stood by the high wall at
the end of the south lawn. Before the war,
when the General's wife was still alive, Mr
Pincher had used the roller to smooth the lawn
for tennis parties and other games. Nothing
ever happened on the south lawn now, even in
summer. The grass was kept short and that
was all.

Dan had a hard time shifting the roller.
It had bedded itself into the earth. He had to
rock it to and fro to loosen it, then pull it out.
Once he'd got the roller free, Dan could move it
more easily, but it was still a tough job for a
boy by himself. He plodded up and down,
sweating in the dim cold morning. The lawn
was flat, but Dan was puzzled to see here and
there what looked like tyre-marks. It looked as

if someone had driven a car here, or maybe a motor-bike. When he'd pushed the roller over the marks once or twice, they vanished. At one spot, something brown seemed to have been spilled on the grass. It was a bit sticky and left a funny smell on Dan's fingers. *I'll tell Mr Pincher*, he thought. But then he remembered what Mr Pincher had said. He'd told Dan to mind his own business. He'd better just forget it.

At half eleven the job was done at last. It was too soon for lunch, so Dan parked the roller and spent the time before lunch picking up twigs and other bits of rubbish that had blown into the garden. He made a big pile of it in the south-east corner of the wall. Maybe Mr Pincher would let him set fire to it sometime. There was nothing Dan liked better than a good bonfire.

He pulled out the silver pocket watch that had belonged to Grandad Terry. It was six minutes to twelve. If he set off now and walked slowly, it'd be bang on midday when he got to the glasshouses. *What's Mrs Pincher put in the sandwiches today?* he asked himself.

"I hope that lawn's as smooth as a bowling green, is it?" asked the gardener, as he plonked the billy on the stove.

"I think so, Mr Pincher," Dan grunted. "Weighs a ton, that roller."

"Wouldn't work if it were like a feather, would it? Here." Mr Pincher gave Dan a sandwich with something pink inside. "Oooh, *Spam*," said Dan. "Wizard."

Pincher snorted. "Dunno about wizard, boy. Nice change from mousetrap, I suppose." Mousetrap was what he called cheese.

"I *love* Spam," said Dan. He looked at the gardener. "My mum says you were a Little Billington Pal, Mr Pincher."

Pincher nodded. "Aye."

"What did you get to eat? In the trenches, I mean."

"Ha!" The gardener made a face. "Bully beef, biscuit, soup now and then. And rum."

"*Rum?*"

"Aye. They'd to get us half-drunk or we'd never have gone over the top."

21

"You were shot in the hand, Mum says."

"Aye, but it were nowt."

"My grandad was a Pal as well. He was killed."

Pincher nodded. "I know. Frank Terry. Good bloke. We was pals at school."

"And the General," said Dan. "Was he your Commanding Officer?"

"Aye," Mr Pincher said.

"And did he get hurt or anything?"

The gardener shook his head. "He wasn't in the trenches, he was with the other generals planning it all. In a chateau – that's a great big posh French house to you."

Dan frowned. "Doesn't seem fair, him in a chateau, his men in the mud. Why doesn't the General like the Home Guard, Mr Pincher?"

"Ah, well now." Pincher looked into the bottom of his mug. "That's a question I'm never going to answer, 'cos you never asked it." He stood up, emptied the mug into a tray of seedlings and wiped his mouth with the back of his hand.

"There's three dozen seedlings in every tray," he went on. "You've three dozen trays to prick out before dark. That's 1,296 plants, so you'd best jump to it, boy."

All the beds and borders along the front of the house were ready. Dan had dug them over a week ago. Seventeen big square windows overlooked these gardens – four on each side of the door, eight upstairs, and one above the door. Each window had eight glass panes, all the same size. It all made a tidy pattern. "Beds and borders got to make a pattern and all," he'd told Dan. "Use pegs and string, plant in dead straight rows."

1,296 plants. In one afternoon, dead straight rows. Dan told himself his mum was right – the General was getting his money's worth.

It felt creepy, working under all those windows. It was as if the house was watching Dan with great square eyes. Dan didn't dare plant a single seedling out of line. He looked up from time to time, but all he could see were the squares of windows and they all just reflected the sky.

He'd nearly finished the first bed when the General's car drove up to the house. It scrunched to a stop. The house doors opened and General Winton came out. Dan kept his head down and pushed in the last few plants. The General's driver opened the car door and touched his grey cap as the General got in. Then the driver limped round to the driver's door. Dan watched as the car pulled away. He daren't look up, because the housekeeper Mrs Burton was on the top step.

The car drove off. Mrs Burton turned and went indoors. Dan knelt up to stretch. Just then he thought he saw something above him. He looked up. A man was standing at one of the bedroom windows. Perhaps from up there he could still see the car. When he saw Dan, the man stepped quickly back, so that a curtain hid him. Dan watched the window, but the man had gone.

Dan shrugged. *Mind your own business*, said a little voice in his head. He picked up his tools and the plants and moved to the next bed.

Chapter 5
Goal-posts on the Slough

Monday morning at Little Billington Elementary School. The top class. Half-way through Maths, the bell went. Dan stood up with everyone else. A bell in the middle of a lesson meant only one thing – shelter drill.

"All right, lead on," growled Mr Shaw. Mr Shaw never liked it when he had to stop his lessons half-way.

The girls and boys didn't mind. Shelter drill gave them a break. It made a change and gave them a chance to stretch their legs. They walked slowly out of the classroom. The back row first, the front row last. The dimmest kids sat on the front row. Everyone said the teachers made them go last because if it was a real air raid, it wouldn't matter all that much if they got killed. This wasn't true, but the bright kids liked to think it was.

The air raid shelter was across the yard. It was a long, red brick building with a thick cement roof. There was a door at each end and no windows. When bombs fall, many of the people who die are killed by flying glass. No windows means no flying glass.

No windows also means darkness. Kids like the dark because teachers can't see in it. They crowded on the long wooden bench, pushing each other and giggling. In the top class, boys tried to find room next to their favourite girls.

When everyone was in the shelter, the teachers called their registers to check no one was missing. Taking the register in the dark, even with a torch, took ages. As a double check, the caretaker looked in every classroom and cloakroom. At last, the Head Teacher would come and say 'well done, everyone', or tell them off, depending on how it had gone.

The Head Teacher was Miss Milsom, and sometimes she'd talk to them for a minute or two. It was fun sitting in the dark, listening to the voice of someone you couldn't see. Better than Maths anyway.

Today she said, "Hands up those of you who have seen one of those posters with the words WALLS HAVE EARS on them?" It wasn't much good saying 'hands up', because she couldn't see the hands. She said it from habit.

"Who can tell us what it means, *Walls Have Ears*? Can *you*, Eric Morley?" Eric Morley was a front row boy. She was sure he wouldn't know.

"No, Miss," said Eric, after he'd thought for a bit.

"What about *you*, Sal Barley?" Sal was back row, top class. "Miss, it means you shouldn't talk about war stuff, because you never know who's listening. There could be a German spy, even if you think there's just you and your friend."

Miss Milsom smiled in the dark. "That's right Sal, well done. Did you hear that, Eric Morley?"

"Yes, Miss," said Eric in a gloomy voice.

Back in the classroom, Dan thought about spies. It was more interesting than long division. The fact that anyone might be a spy was exciting. You didn't have to be in the Army to meet the enemy. You could brush against someone who was a spy when you were waiting for the bus. The trick was to *know* he was a spy. There must be *something* not quite right about a spy – some little thing that'd give him away. Dan made up his mind to look at people more carefully from now on.

Winter evenings dragged a bit. The black-out made it dangerous to be out. Cars and lorries had hoods over their head-lamps. In the dark you could easily be knocked down. Then there was the Home Guard. Many of the men weren't fully trained, and they were jumpy about spies and enemy agents. Sometimes they'd shoot at shapes in the dark before they knew what they really were. Not long ago a boy on a bike had been shot dead near an aircraft factory. Dan's mother read about it in the paper, and after that she didn't want him to go out after dark.

"Aw *Mu-um*," he begged that Monday after tea. "I'm at school all day and working all weekend – I need *some* fun. Let me go out for an hour. Just an hour. I won't take the bike, and I'll be home at seven on the dot, I promise."

At last his mother let him go, and Dan made his way to the Slough. The Slough was some marshy ground that belonged to General Winton. It was too wet for cattle or sheep, and too wet to grow food on, even in wartime. It might have made a good training ground for the Home Guard, but the General had said they were not to train on any of his land. No one walked on the Slough, even in daylight. Only Dan went there at night.

It was a good place to play at war. It would be more fun with pals of course, but Dan hadn't many friends. The village kids played together at weekends, when he was at work. He wasn't in anyone's gang. It made him a bit of a loner.

He found a tree branch that looked a bit like a rifle. It was all he needed for a game of war. That, and his imagination.

German paratroops had landed on the Slough. No one knew except Rifleman Langley. He had to destroy them now, while they were shedding their parachutes and getting their equipment together.

Langley was a brilliant fighter. He hid behind a mound of earth, then darted behind another one and shot out again. He moved so swiftly and so silently, that the Germans thought they were surrounded by British troops. Their commander told his men to lay down their guns and surrender. The Germans worked out too late that there was only one soldier attacking them. They'd surrendered and Rifleman Langley marched them at gun point into the village. A band played, and people stood by the road cheering. He gave the Germans over to the Home Guard at the village hall.

In real life Little Billington had no band and it was night time. How would anyone have known Dan was coming? But that didn't worry him at all. In games and dreams, there's no need to explain.

Playing his game had meant Dan was close to the high wall round Winton Hall now. Behind this bit of it lay the south lawn and the old orangery. Dan thought it must be seven o'clock by now, and he was turning to go home when he saw something odd. A line of tiny, gleaming studs had been set into the wall. They ran from near the ground to the top, then along. He followed the line of studs. They were four feet above his head and hard to see in the dark. After about forty yards they ended and there was another vertical line going down to the ground. He touched one of the studs with his finger. It was cold and smooth, like half a marble.

What are they? Dan asked himself. *What're they for? Could they be to do with the war in some way?* It was really dark now and Dan had to set off home. *Goal-posts*, he thought. *They're like a set of goal-posts for a giant goalie.* He grinned. *Maybe there's a monster out here – The Giant Goalie of the Slough.*

Chapter 6
Walls Have Eyes

For the rest of that week, Dan spent a lot of time thinking about the weird studs he'd found in the wall. It was hard to pay attention to his lessons. He made up this poem –

The studs in the wall
At Winton Hall.

Not much of a poem to start with, but he added to it as the week went on:

The studs in the wall
At Winton Hall
Where some great monster
Kicks a ball.

Good, that. Another version went like this:

The studs in the wall
At Winton Hall
Are not about
The war at all.

Not as good somehow, and anyway Dan thought the studs *did* have something to do with the war.

But what?

After tea on Friday, he went to the Slough for another look. The sky wasn't as dark as it had been on Monday. Dan could see more. He saw that the studs were set in fresh cement. There was moss all over the wall but none on the cement, so it hadn't been there very long. Someone had slapped on cement, then pressed the studs into it while it was soft. But *why*?

He took out the jack-knife his dad had given him on his last leave from the Navy. *Let's get a closer look at one of these things*, Dan thought. *Whoever put 'em here won't miss one.* He chose a stud that was just above his head, and hacked at the cement that held it in place. The stuff fell away as grains and powder. A metal tube fell out of the wall. Dan picked it up. At the end of the tube was something like a little glass ball.

As soon as Dan had it in his hand, he knew what it was. It was a cat's eye – one of those reflector studs on the road that help people drive at night. He frowned. *Why would someone set lines of cat's eyes in a wall, for Pete's sake? Does it have something to do with the war? Perhaps I shouldn't have seen them. Mr Pincher'd tell me to mind my own business.*

It was a quarter to seven. He'd got home late on Monday and Mum had snapped at him. Better try to be early tonight. He closed the knife, slipped it into his pocket with the cat's eye, and set off home.

"Daniel?" It was supper time. They were sipping their cocoa. His mother had been watching him.

"Yes, Mum?" Dan said.

"What're you thinking about? You've been miles away."

"Oh, nothing really," Dan told her.

"You've been thinking about *something*, love. What is it?"

"All right." Dan fished in his pocket. "Know what this is?"

"Yes, of course," said his mum. "It's a cat's eye. Did you find it at the roadside? They sometimes come loose."

Dan shook his head. "No, I dug it out of the General's wall. There's hundreds of them, they make a shape like goal-posts."

"How odd," said Dan's mum. "What can they be for?"

Dan shrugged. "That's what I've been thinking about," he said.

His mother made a face. "Well, let's hope they're not important to the war effort, as you've pinched one. Don't want you arrested, do we?"

Dan shook his head. "I don't think they'll miss *one*, Mum. Anyway," he grinned, "next time Miss Milsom says anything about walls having ears, I'll tell her *I* know a wall that has *eyes*."

Cocoa helps you sleep, but it didn't help Dan that night. He lay on his back, watching ghostly shapes in the dark.

Cat's eyes, he thought. *No use in the daytime. Only at night, when head-lamps shine into them. They reflect back the light, and that's what makes 'em shine. But what light will ever shine on those cat's eyes? No one drives a car onto the Slough. No one even walks there with a torch. And if they did, and lit up the goal-posts, what would be the point? It's just a bit of blank wall.*

Around midnight an aeroplane flew over, high above the house. Dan tensed and listened to the lonely drone of its engine. "Let it be one of ours," he whispered. "And if it is, keep it safe."

As the engine noise faded away, a thought came to him. It was a crazy thought, the sort that crosses your mind when you're half asleep. It made his heart beat a bit faster, but he shook his head on the pillow and turned over. *In the morning, when I'm awake I'll know what a stupid thought that is*, he told himself. *That's if I remember anything about it at all.*

He drifted off to sleep and dreamed he was a sailor, on a railway station, saying goodbye to Miss Milsom.

He remembered his crazy thought the moment he woke up. It wasn't crazy at all. In fact it fitted in with the other things he'd noticed last week, when he was rolling the south lawn. He got out of bed. It was Saturday and only half past six. Mum wasn't up yet, but Dan wanted to set off for Winton Hall early. There was stuff he needed to check out before he started work and met Mr Pincher in the glasshouse – stuff he didn't want the gardener to know about. Not yet, anyway.

He got dressed and was just putting on his shoes when his mum came downstairs in her dressing-gown and curlers. He told her Mr Pincher had asked him to start work early today. "Huh!" she grunted. "And will they add a few coppers to your wages, d'you think? For the extra work?"

Dan made a face. "Not much hope of that, Mum."

"No – I agree, love. If you've no time for breakfast, at least take some bread and cheese to eat on the way."

Dan biked off up the lane with a hunk of bread in his fist, a cube of cheese in one pocket and the cat's eye in the other. When he got to the gates of Winton Hall he didn't turn in. He hid the bike behind a bush and set off to walk along the outside of the high wall. The Slough began where the wall turned a corner. The ground was marshy here. Dan tried to dodge the big puddles. Soon he was at the first line of cat's eyes – the ones which went up from the ground towards the top of the wall. It was time to test his crazy idea.

He looked all around to make sure no one was about, then climbed the wall. He wasn't going to drop over into the grounds, he just needed to see the view from the top. When he did, his heart speeded up a bit, as it had last night in bed. He dropped back onto the Slough and trudged the forty yards to where the other goal-post was. He climbed the wall again and peeped over. It was just as he had thought.

He started to make his way back to the gates. Should he tell Mr Pincher what he'd worked out? *Might have worked out*, he told himself. Might *have*. *It's early days, still too soon to be sure. We'll have to wait and see.*

Chapter 7
Jigsaw

Dan hadn't managed to plant out all of the 1,296 plants last weekend, so he knew what he'd be doing today. At quarter past eight he was kneeling once more in front of all those windows. He looked up from time to time, but didn't see anyone watching.

He'd been working for an hour when he heard Sal Barley singing. She was round the side of the house. He thought he'd go and say good morning to her. If the gardener checked up and found him skiving, too bad. Dan was beginning to think there were worse things than *that* going on at Winton Hall.

"Morning, Sal," he said.

"Oh, it's *you*," said Sal. "I hope you've not come to ask more of your cheeky questions. Mrs Burton heard you last week and told me off."

"Ah." Dan nodded. "I *knew someone* had ratted on me to Mr Pincher ..." He looked at the clothes line. "Not so many sheets today, eh, Sal?"

"Ssssh!" Sal looked towards the kitchen door. "Shut your gob, Dan Langley, you'll get us *both* the sack." She pulled a shirt out of her basket. "You better go anyway – I've got to finish this, then help Mum get a room ready. General's got an important guest coming tonight."

"*Has* he?" murmured Dan. "Who is it, Sal?"

"How should *I* know?" growled Sal. "Go back to your work and let me get on with mine."

Dan nodded. "Fair enough, Sal. Don't work too hard."

Back on his knees, Dan pushed the plants into the ground and thought about all the different things he'd seen. All the bits of random information were like pieces of a jigsaw puzzle. Now he had to fit them all together. *Tyre tracks in the south lawn, and an oil stain.*

Too many sheets, which someone didn't like him counting.

Cat's eyes in the shape of goal-posts that mark exactly where the south lawn starts and finishes and a cross-bar to show how high the wall is.

And the General's got an important guest coming tonight.

Dan sighed and shook his head. He couldn't fit all the bits of information together. It was still a puzzle – but a very interesting one.

He pressed in the last plant, picked up his stuff and went to report to Mr Pincher. It wasn't lunchtime yet, but Mr Pincher was so happy to have all the front planted, he let Dan sit down and gave him a mug of tea.

They worked together through the afternoon and knocked off at five. As Dan bent to fit his bike-clips Mr Pincher walked over to him. "Don't forget to turn your money over tonight, boy," he said.

Dan stood up. "Turn my *money* over? What d'you *mean*, Mr Pincher?"

"The money in your *pocket*, lad. It's new moon tonight, if you turn your money over, they say more'll come to you."

Dan grinned. "Load of rubbish, Mr Pincher, if you ask me. And anyway, *what* money? I won't have any till you pay me and that's tomorrow."

He was half-way home before he worked out that he'd found another piece for his jigsaw.

It was macaroni cheese for tea. Dan didn't like macaroni cheese, but today he didn't care what he ate. It could have been worms in a tomato sauce and he'd have shovelled 'em down. He was busy fitting the latest bit of information into his jigsaw.

General's got an important guest coming tonight. And it's new moon.

"Mum?" Dan asked.

"What is it, love?"

"Mr Pincher reckons it's new moon tonight. That means no moon at all, doesn't it?" Dan wanted to be sure.

"Yes it does, Dan. And tomorrow there'll be the thinnest slice, what people call a sickle moon."

"So it'll be really dark tonight?" Dan checked.

"As dark as it ever gets, love." She frowned. "Why?"

"Oh, nothing, Mum. Pincher says I should turn my money over."

"Daft so-and-so. Better if he turned more of his money over to you."

Dan got into bed that night with his clothes on. He thought something might happen at the

Hall tonight, and he wanted to be there if it did.

This is what he'd worked out.

An aeroplane. The cat's eyes are there to guide an aeroplane as it comes into land. They must be. If a pilot wanted to land on the south lawn at night, what would he need to know? He'd need to know how high the wall was so as not to crash into it as he landed. And he'd need to know exactly where the south lawn was. The lines on the wall aren't goal-posts. They'd show a pilot both those things. I must be right, mustn't I? What else could the cat's eyes be for?

Dan wished he could go to the Police House and tell Constable White, but he knew it would be no good. It isn't enough just to *think* something fishy's going on. Especially if you think an important person like the General is mixed up in it. You need proof. The village policeman wouldn't even come and *look* at the cat's eyes.

No. This was something Dan must do by himself.

He heard his mother go to bed. He waited half an hour, then crept downstairs and slipped outside.

The night was cold and clear. The stars were out, but there was no moon. It was eleven o'clock. Dan saw no one as he walked to the Slough. He had on his jacket, the thick trousers and boots he wore for gardening, and a scarf. He carried a black-out torch, and the Box Brownie camera his grandma had given him for his birthday. *Hope there won't be an air raid*, he thought. *Mum'll be frantic if the siren goes off and I'm not there.*

He leaned on the wall near the cat's eyes. It was freezing. Every few minutes he pulled out his grandad's watch and shone the torch on it. *Half past eleven. Ten to twelve. Five past midnight. Crikey, it's cold. Nothing's happening. Maybe I'm wrong. I'll give it till half one, then I'm off*, he thought.

He walked up and down to warm himself. Forty steps to the far post. Turn. Forty steps back to the near post. Turn. Forty steps …

At half past one, nothing had happened. *Five more minutes*, he told himself.

Ten minutes passed. Fifteen. Dan couldn't drag himself away. At ten to two, he thought he heard something. He held his breath, and listened. There was a thin buzz, like a bee. He crouched and stared into the dark, trying to see if anything was there. There was nothing to see except stars, but the noise was coming closer. *It's an aeroplane*, he thought. *It can't be anything else.*

His heart pounded at his ribs. *Was I right after all?* He could hardly believe it.

He was still staring into the night when a flash dazzled him. He jerked his head to the side and watched as a brilliant light sped towards him, twenty feet up in the air. He looked at the wall and saw the goal-posts and cross-bar drawn in points of light. A second later a shadow blotted out the stars, the cat's eyes went out and a gust of wind pushed over his head. The buzzing cut off. Green blobs floated in front of Dan's eyes.

He knew he hadn't long, he must act now. He stood up and felt for finger holds in the wall. He began to climb. The Box Brownie was heavy in his pocket. It made the climb harder.

47

He reached the top and peered down the south lawn. The green blobs were fading. He could just see the aeroplane. There was a dim glow where its cabin was, a streak of light fell on a strut and he made out the underside of a wing. Someone was moving there with a hooded torch.

He could hear voices but not what they said. There were three or four people. He hardly dared breathe. Whatever they were doing, they didn't want anyone else to see. He longed to drop down off the wall and run away, but first he must take the photo.

The camera click was nothing, but it sounded to Dan like a thunder-clap. He dropped at once, holding the Brownie tight. No shout came from beyond the wall. Dan turned and fled.

Chapter 8
Wasting Police Time

Dan wanted a lie-in Sunday morning, but it wasn't on. He must act normally. Breakfast with Mum. Bike to the Hall. Work. Not a word to anyone. Walls have ears.

The camera lay under some junk in his wardrobe. He'd get the film developed by Mr Halliday the chemist, but not today.

The proof was on that film, Dan hoped. A photo taken at night with a Box Brownie wouldn't show much. *All I need is the rough shape of an aeroplane*, he told himself as he got out of bed.

Dan knew what sort of an aeroplane it was. Last year he'd swapped a police whistle for a pack of cards with pictures of planes on them. There were fifty-two cards. Each card showed a different plane. Some were enemy planes. Some were friendly. The name of the plane was on the back of the card. Sailors, soldiers and airmen had to know each plane without looking at the name. If they knew them all, they'd know if planes they saw in the sky were enemies or friends. They'd shoot at enemy planes, not friends.

Dan had laid the cards out on the kitchen table hundreds of times. He could name most of them without turning the cards over. The plane he'd seen on the south lawn was a Fieseler Storch. Storch is Stork in German. It was an enemy plane, famous because it could land on short rough runways, such as fields or lawns.

Dan's plan was to take his photo to Constable White. If the policeman saw the photo of the German plane, that'd be proof that General Winton was letting an enemy aircraft use his south lawn. The police'd have to act.

Dan knew he'd have his photos by Friday or Saturday. He had to wait till then.

One thing worried him. If the General was arrested, Dan was certain to lose his job at the Hall. He knew his mum needed his weekly four bob to put food on the table. But there was a war on and everyone had to put duty before everything, didn't they? Mr Pincher would lose his job too, come to that, and Sal's mum. General in prison, empty hall, no work. But Dan remembered what his dad used to say, 'When in doubt, carry on.' Dan knew he had to carry on.

He took his camera film to Halliday's on Monday. The rest of the week seemed to last forever. *BE LIKE DAD, KEEP MUM* said a poster he walked past every day. 'Keep mum' means keep quiet. He was learning how terribly hard it is to keep a really important secret.

Friday crawled round at last, and Dan went to collect his photos. "That'll be one and threepence," said the chemist. He looked at Dan. "I don't know why you bothered, son. There's only one picture, and *that's* just shadows." He shook his head. "Tell you what –

give me sixpence and we'll call it quits." He smiled. "You can't do night photography with a Box Brownie, lad. You'll have to save up and get a *proper* camera."

Outside, Dan took the snapshot out of its envelope. It *was* shadows, but he thought he could just make out the Storch. The negative of the photo was a bit better. On the negative dark was light and light dark. There was an aeroplane shape *there* all right. He pedalled to the Police House.

Constable White answered the door himself. "Yes lad – what can I do for *you?*"

Dan had practised what he was going to say. "I'm Daniel Langley," he said. "I work weekends at Winton Hall, in the gardens. Something's going on there. An enemy aeroplane lands on the south lawn."

"Oh, aye?" The policeman's lips twitched in a short smile. "And I suppose storm-troopers get out and march off towards London, eh?"

"No, it's a *light* plane. Look." Dan pulled out the envelope. "I took this picture, Saturday night. It was new moon." He held out the photo.

The constable looked hard at the photo and then handed it back. "You're pulling my leg, lad, there's nothing on it. Run along now – my tea's getting cold, and I like my spam fritters hot."

"But, *sir*, there's cat's eyes ..." Dan tried to say.

"Go home, son, before I get *really* cross and run you in for wasting police time."

Dan watched the door close. He couldn't believe it. The constable hadn't even seen the negative. "It's a Storch!" he muttered. "A Fieseler Storch."

On his way home, he thought he'd ask his mum what to do, but he changed his mind. *She'd have a fit if she knew I'd been creeping around in the middle of the night*, he thought. *And she'd say the same as Constable White about my photo.*

No – there had to be another way.

Tea was scrambled eggs on toast, made with powdered eggs. Mum said, "I bumped into Mr Carpenter today. Told him you'd asked about joining the Home Guard. He says you have to be sixteen."

"Oh." Mr Carpenter was one of the people in the Home Guard. "That's that, then," said Dan.

The Home Guard. Dan gulped down a mouthful of watery egg. *What if I tell them what I've seen, show 'em my photo? I bet they'll take notice.*

After tea he said, "All right if I go for a ride around, Mum? I shan't be long."

"Be careful," said his mother. "It's getting dark."

The Little Billington Home Guard met every evening in the church hall. Dan got there at quarter past six. There was a sentry with a battered old rifle. "I've come to see the Captain," Dan told him.

"Oh, aye?" The sentry sounded just like Constable White. "Captain Chivers is busy, lad. You can't just push your way in here ..."

"It's urgent," Dan butted in. "I've got a photo the Captain will want to see."

"Wait here."

Dan waited. After a minute the sentry came back. "Follow me," he said. They crossed the hall, where Sergeant Carpenter was drilling a squad of men. The sentry knocked on a door and opened it, then left Dan on his own. Captain Chivers looked at Dan across his desk. "You wanted to see me, boy – something about a photograph?"

"Yes, sir."

"Show me," Captain Chivers said.

Dan slid the photo across the desk. Captain Chivers looked at it for a few minutes. "What's this supposed to show, laddie?"

"It's a Fieseler Storch, sir. On the south lawn at Winton Hall. Last Saturday night. It was new moon, sir."

"A Fieseler *Storch*?" The captain frowned. "The Storch is an enemy aircraft. What would an enemy aircraft be doing at Winton Hall?"

"I don't know, sir, but I saw it land. There are cat's eyes, sir, set into the wall. They mark the height of the wall, and the position of the lawn. I can show you, sir."

"Can you indeed?" Captain Chivers was still looking at the photo. "I can't really *see* an aircraft on this, let alone be sure what type it is. I don't think ..."

"Look, sir, this is the negative." Dan pushed the square of film across the desk. "It shows up better."

Captain Chivers looked at the negative. "Hmmm ... it's a tiny bit better, I suppose." He looked up. "Did you say something about cat's eyes, laddie?"

"Yes, sir, set in the wall. I dug one out, I've got it here."

The captain looked at the cat's eye. He asked Dan a few questions, then said, "All right, laddie, I'll tell you what I'll do. I'm going to show your photo to a man I know. He's in the Airforce, works with aerial photos. If anyone can work out what you've snapped, it's him. And I'll send a patrol out to look at these cat's eyes of yours. All right?"

Dan's heart kicked him in the ribs. "Yes, sir, thank you, sir.

I ... don't suppose I could go with the patrol, sir, as a sort of guide ..."

"Certainly *not*," growled the captain, "this isn't the wild west." He relaxed, smiled. "Thank you, Master Langley, for ... all you've done. I'll let you know in due course if anything comes of this."

Chapter 9

A Good Bonfire

In due course. Dan waited. February turned into March. He kept 'mum'. *The man Captain Chivers knows will have had a good look at my photo*, he told himself. *He'll know that plane was a Storch. Any day now they'll arrest General Winton. It'll be in the papers, how I did my bit for my country.*

A week passed. Two weeks. Nothing happened. He biked up to Winton Hall Saturdays and Sundays, and everything was the same. He did his jobs for Mr Pincher. The General came and went. Sal Barley pegged out the washing. Mr Pincher nagged him. Dan got his four shillings and took them home to his mother.

The third week in March Dan said to himself, *they're not going to do anything. The airforce chap couldn't see the Storch. They think the cat's eyes don't mean anything special. General Winton's getting away with it.*

He lay in bed, thinking. *Looks as if it's up to me*, he thought. *I'll have to take action myself, stop whatever's going on up there.* The idea scared him. He'd be taking on dangerous people. Traitors. Enemy agents. Killing one boy would be nothing to them – like squashing a beetle. *But I've got to do it*, he told himself. *My Duty. Dad did his duty, and so must I.*

At breakfast he said, "When will it be new moon again, Mum?"

"*Why*, Daniel?" His mother was worried about him. He wasn't talking much anymore, as if there was something on his mind.

"Oh," Dan grinned, "I thought I'd have another go at turning my money over."

His mother shook her head. "That's just a silly story, love – the only way to get money is to work for it." She looked him in the eye. "Do you *need* money for something, Daniel? Are you in any sort of trouble?"

He shook his head. "No, Mum, of *course* I'm not in trouble. I was just asking."

"Well, new moon last month was on the 26th, so this month it'll be on the 27th."

"One day later?"

She nodded. "That's how it works."

And that's when the Storch'll come again, he told himself. *Darkest night of the month. Makes sense. I'll be there again, and this time I'll do something about it.*

He'd do *something* about it, but he'd no idea what.

It was waiting time again. *'Keep mum'* time. Dan hated it. He was dying to tell someone. His mother. Or Miss Milsom at school. Or even Mr Pincher, but he knew that none of them would believe him. An old English General, helping Nazi agents? Stupid.

60

Mr Pincher might even *tell* the General, and who knows what'd happen *then?*

As March 27th drew near, Dan felt worse. He was worried. He couldn't concentrate on his school work. He didn't sleep well. All the time he was trying to find a way to wriggle out of the vow he'd made. He'd promised himself he'd do something about it.

Why should I? he asked himself. *I tried to tell people. I risked my life to get proof. They didn't believe me. What more can I do?*

But it was no good. Every night and every morning, he looked at his dad's photo by his bed. "When in doubt," it seemed to say, "carry on." It had been Able Seaman Langley's motto.

On March 27th, the new moon, Dan said goodnight to his mother and went to bed in his clothes. At midnight he got up, whispered "Wish me luck," to his dad's picture, and slipped out.

The night was damp and chilly. It was the winter's end and the Slough had more puddles than before. By the time he got to the wall, Dan's socks were sodden. He shivered, partly with cold, partly because of what he was planning to do.

He knew it was no good staying outside the wall. He'd see the cat's eyes shine, feel the gust of air as the Storch skimmed over his head. But *then* what?

Tonight he had to be *on the south lawn* when the aeroplane arrived. And someone would see him. They'd catch him for sure, maybe even kill him. But he hoped he'd have done what he'd planned before then.

He climbed the wall and looked over. Nothing moved on the lawn, there were no lights in the orangery. He dropped down onto the lawn and froze. No dog barked. No light came on. He moved along the wall, round to where he'd parked the great roller. There was a narrow gap between the roller and the wall. Dan squeezed into it. If he crouched, no one'd see him there.

His grandad's watch said it was quarter past one. If the Storch came at the same time, he'd still have thirty-five minutes to wait. Long, cold, scary minutes. *And that's if the Storch comes at all*, he told himself.

At half past one, nothing had happened. *It's not coming*, thought Dan. *I guessed wrong*. Then, at twenty-five to two, he saw something move behind the dirty glass of the orangery. A light. Shadowy figures.

Dan crouched, his heart thumping. The orangery door opened with a creak. Someone was standing there, smoking. He could see the glowing tip of a cigarette. A line from a song came to him, a song about cigarettes –

> *A fire on one end,*
> *And a fool on the other.*

He hoped the chap on the end of *that* cigarette was a fool – too big a fool to catch Dan.

He strained his ears. He daren't look at his watch, but it must be about time. He moved as softly as he could. He gripped the roller's wooden handle with both hands. And then he heard it at last – that thin, insect buzz. It was now.

His whole body quivered. The timing had to be perfect. Move too soon, and the pilot would see and be warned. He wouldn't land the plane and Dan would be caught anyway. If he moved too late – then all this wait and worry would be wasted. *Wait for the light*, he told himself. *The light*.

The Storch skimmed across the countryside. As it reached the Slough, the pilot switched on the plane's powerful lamp. The cat's eyes shone. The pilot lifted the plane's nose so as to clear the wall. The man in the passenger seat screwed his eyes shut.

Dan heaved the heavy roller into the middle of the lawn. They saw him at once. Dan heard swearing. The smoker flung his cigarette away and came running. A second man waved a hooded torch at the plane to warn the pilot. Dan ran back to the wall, but he knew he'd never reach it in time.

At the last second the pilot saw the warning torch, but it was too late. The Storch landed, bounced, and piled into the roller with a splintering crash. Dan knew the two men inside would have been killed instantly. The man who was chasing Dan swerved out of the plane's way. Dan reached the foot of the wall. The plane exploded in flames and lit up the

Hall and the south lawn. It was as if someone
had shone a huge searchlight. Dan knew he
was caught. He closed his eyes. The man
chasing him took aim with an automatic pistol.
Dan closed his eyes. No way could the man
miss.

"Drop the gun!" At the sound of that
command, Dan opened his eyes. The south
lawn was swarming with men in uniform. Two
of them pointed rifles at the gunman. He flung
down the pistol and raised his hands. Dan saw
a cursing figure dragged out of the orangery.
It was General Winton.

Someone strode towards Dan. "Are you all
right, laddie?" he shouted. It was Captain
Chivers. Dan grinned. "Yes I am, sir, thanks to
you and your men."

The Captain shook his head. "Don't thank
us Daniel. It's thanks to you we're here at all –
you and your Box Brownie. He smiled. "Does
your mother know you're out?"

Dan smiled. "I hope not, sir," he said.

The Captain went back to his men and left
Dan to watch the plane burn. There was
nothing Dan liked better than a good bonfire.

Our books are tested
for children and young people by
children and young people.

Thanks to everyone who consulted on
a manuscript for their time and effort in
helping us to make our books better
for our readers.